Willy was having the time of his life!

Then . . . I saw it. A white pickup stopped at the edge of the baseball field. It had cages in the back and a flashing blue light on top. A man got out. From the back of the truck, he picked up a long pole with a rope noose on the end.

It was the pound!

I felt sick.

If I didn't do something—and quick—Willy was going to be in so much trouble. . . .

But if I went to rescue him—to make him give the ball back and run and hide before the man from the pound came—then Roscoe and Rikki would know that I had a *dog* for a friend. They wouldn't like me anymore.

Willy flew like a rocket around the field, right toward where we were sitting on the fence. The man from the pound came from the other direction. . . .

Willy didn't even see him. He was watching the boys who chased him. If Willy didn't look up, he was a goner!

BILL WALLACE

UPCHUCK and the ROTTEN WILLY
Running Wild

A
MINSTREL®
BOOK

Published by POCKET BOOKS
New York   London   Toronto   Sydney   Singapore

A MINSTREL PAPERBACK *Original*

A Minstrel Book published by
POCKET BOOKS, a division of Simon & Schuster, Inc.
1230 Avenue of the Americas, New York, NY 10020

Text copyright © 2000 by Bill Wallace
Illustrations copyright © 2000 by John Steven Gurney

ISBN: 0-7434-0027-5

First Minstrel Books printing October 2000

Published simultaneously in hardcover by Minstrel Books

10 9 8 7 6 5 4 3 2 1

A MINSTREL BOOK and colophon are registered trademarks of Simon & Schuster, Inc.

Cover art by John Steven Gurney

Printed in the U.S.A.

With deep appreciation to:

Pam Charlson, Cathy and Don Simer
and to
Cheryl Green, Peggy Horrell, Alice Hurry,
Beth Ann Meyer, and Verdeana Weidenmaier

Running Wild

CHAPTER 1

Okay . . . it was weird.

The people out in the field were weird. The people sitting on the cement steps were weird. And Willy—well . . . he was weirdest!

My people went to the kitchen to eat. These people ate on the cement steps. My people listened to music and visited. These people yelled and other people threw them food. In return, they gave them little pieces of paper. These people would seem fine, then all of a sudden they would leap to their feet and yell at the top of their lungs. They would clap and . . .

"Willy, no!"

. . . and they would jump up and act really mad. Then just as quickly as they started, they'd sit down and eat and talk some more.

The people out in the grass were just as bad. They talked and jabbered all the time. They wore shirts, tight pants with long socks, and little caps on their heads. Right now most of them had blue caps and white pants. There was only one, standing on a little bag, who had on a red cap and gray pants. But just a moment ago it was the other way around and . . .

"Willy, quit!"

. . . and most of the boys had on these big gloves. That was weird because they were lots bigger than the gloves my people wore in the wintertime. But what was even weirder was that they only wore one glove instead of two. People had two front paws—I mean hands—so why only one glove? Maybe the other hand just didn't get cold.

The glove was so big, they couldn't pick up stuff with it on. They couldn't pick their noses or scratch. About the only thing they could do was catch the ball that they threw at one another. One boy stood on a pillow. He didn't have a glove. Fact was, he didn't have anything except his pants and shirt and . . .

"Willy, cool it!"

. . . and shoes and red cap. But another boy, who was dressed just like him, had on a hard hat and a big stick in his hand. It wasn't a very good stick. The thing was wide and sort of swollen on one end and kind of narrow on the other end.

One of the boys who wore a blue cap kept throwing a ball at the guy in the red cap. He wasn't a very good thrower, because he hardly ever hit anybody. Sometimes he did get close, and the boy with the stick would use it to whack at the ball so it wouldn't hit him. Another boy, who was really short, would throw the ball back so he could try again.

Usually everybody missed. The thrower missed the guy with the stick, and the guy with the stick missed the ball and . . .

"Willy, don't even think about it!"

. . . and this big man in a black suit behind the little short guy would yell: "Strike!" When that happened, people on the steps would stop eating long enough to yell at him. Then the whole thing would start all over again.

Weird!

I guess the boys standing out in the grass wanted to play with the ball, too. They were always watching it. When they weren't watching, they would yell stuff like:

"Batter, batter, batter, BATTER, SWING!" And other times they would yell: "Easy out. Easy out."

Mostly, they just chewed their gum or blew bubbles and they spit a lot and . . .

"Willy! Would you quit it!"

. . . and they scratched a lot, too. I guess they had fleas. I had a flea once. The thing sure itched. I probably scratched as much as they did.

Willy and I sat beside this big, long trench in the ground. It was made of hard, gray blocks and had a metal roof. Sometimes when it was really hot, Willy would dig a hole or a trench and we'd lay in it to cool off. These boys weren't trying to cool off, though. They were busy yelling at the boys on the grass—especially the guy who was throwing the ball at their friend. They'd called out things like "We want a pitcher, not a belly-itcher." Other times they would yell at the man behind the little short boy—especially if he shouted, "Strike."

They would yell back at him, "Ball."

Like I said—weird.

The ball . . . well, that was what made Willy weird. I mean, it was driving *him* nuts!

And Willy—he was driving *me* nuts!

Willy never took his eyes off of the ball. We were fine as long as someone was holding it or if it was in the air. But if the ball ever hit the ground . . .

All I'd done since we got here was yell and fuss at Willy. As far as I was concerned, this baseball stuff wasn't that much fun.

The boy with the stick whacked at the ball. I guess he figured it was going to hit him, so he swung really hard. A loud *crack* sound came to my ears. The ball hit the ground. A little puff of dust exploded, and the other boy in the red cap, who was standing on the bag, had to jump so the ball didn't hit him.

Sure enough . . . Willy's muscles tensed. His enormous chest quivered and his legs trembled. The ball was headed the other direction—going away from us—but it was all I could do to keep my friend from chasing after it.

I jumped up and put my paws against his shoulder.

"Willy, knock it off!"

The way he was shaking and the way his muscles tensed—ready to spring after the rolling ball— well, this time . . . I didn't know if I could hold him or not.

Luckily, the boy in the blue cap picked up the ball.

Willy sank down on his haunches. He was still panting, his long tongue dangling from his slobbery mouth, his eyes wide and excited. But he sat down. With a heavy sigh, I sat down beside him.

"Willy? I think it's time to go back home, don't you?"

His big, brown eyes never left the ball. Even sitting down, I could see his stub tail wagging—stirring the dust behind and underneath him. When he didn't answer, it made my tail flip.

"Willy? Are you listening to me?"

He gave a slight nod. My tail jerked the other direction. "Willy!"

"Yes," he answered. "I'm listening." He tried to look down at me and keep his eyes on the ball at the same time. I leaned over and rubbed my cheek against his arm.

"Let's go home, please. If you get their ball, it's going to make them mad. They might call 'The Pound!' And we don't want that, do we?"

He shook his head, but he still wouldn't look at me. It was irritating, to say the least. Now my tail was jerking back and forth so hard that I could barely sit.

"I mean it, Willy. You're gonna get us in trouble. I'll leave you. I'll go home without you. I'm serious."

"Okay. Just a second." Like he was in a trance or something, his eyes never left the ball. "Just let me see this one more pitch, then we'll . . ."

"CRACK!"

The little, round ball came flying right in front of the trench where we stood. Willy took off!

It was amazing how something that huge and clunky looking could move so fast. It was like watching an enormous black streak of lightning.

One second he was sitting there beside me, trembling and all excited. The next second he was gone! All that was left was a cloud of dust as he chased after the rolling ball.

The boys with the blue hats yelled at him. The boys with the red hats yelled at him, too. The man in the black suit just shook his head.

Now you've done it! I thought to myself. *Now they're going to call the pound and the guy will catch you and drag you away and . . . and . . . this time I won't be able to save you.*

CHAPTER 2

I'm sorry," he whimpered.

My tail flipped, but I didn't even bother to look at him.

"Yeah, right."

"Honest. I didn't mean to. I just couldn't help myself. My boy used to play catch with me. I loved it. He would throw the ball and I'd chase it. Then he'd chase me and try to get the ball back so he could throw it again and . . . well . . . when that ball came rolling toward me . . . I'm sorry. I just couldn't help it."

My tail flipped so hard, it yanked my rump halfway off the ground. I stood and wheeled around to glare up at him.

"It was embarrassing, Willy," I hissed. "That boy chasing you and yelling. You—running around like an idiot—holding that stupid ball in your mouth as high as you could and slobbering all over it. What if someone had called that man from the pound?"

Willy's head kind of ducked. His ears folded forward, real sheepish like. "I didn't think about that."

"Didn't think about it? Didn't think about it! No kidding. You didn't *think* at all. That's the problem."

His enormous head hung so low, his chin almost bumped the ground. An eyebrow arched. He looked at me with those big, sad brown eyes.

"I won't do it again. Promise. Don't be mad at me."

I took a deep breath. I wanted to hiss at him. I wanted to spit and meow at the top of my lungs. Then, when I looked at those sad eyes and his giant head hanging so low and looking so helpless . . . well, the air just sort of whooshed out of me. The fur along my backbone gave a little ripple.

"Oh, come on," I hissed, softly. "Let's go see what's going on at Luigi's."

We stepped from our hiding place beside the two trash cans at the back of Willy's fence. I peeked around the corner. There was no one there. Willy trotted behind me to the street. We stopped and looked both ways. It was to make sure no cars were coming and to make sure the white truck

with the blue light on top was no place around. I
didn't like that guy from the pound—not one little
bit. Once certain the coast was clear, we crossed
the road and headed for Luigi's Italian Restaurant.
Willy followed so close behind, I could feel his
huge, heavy paws shaking the ground beneath my
feet. Even the thought of spaghetti and meatballs
didn't seem to help. I couldn't keep from thinking
about how I got myself mixed up with this dippy
dog. I guess the whole thing started about two
years ago. In my mind's eye I could still see it as
clear as yesterday.

Tom had been my best friend for as long as I
could remember. He was the cat who lived across
the street. We played chase and explored and
hunted mice. There was a huge pecan tree in his
backyard. Sometimes we climbed out on the limbs
over Rocky's yard and pestered the mean, nasty
Doberman who lived next door.

New neighbors moved in on the other side of
Rocky. They had this enormous black beast in
their backyard. There was a little confusion when
we first met him. He told us he was a Rott (which
was short for Rottweiler) and his name was Willy.
Rott 'n' Willy. Tom and I thought he wasn't a dog
at all. We thought he was some strange monster
called a Rotten Willy.

Tom and I had a friend named Louie. He was an

alley cat. We used to sit on the fence at the track around this grassy field with stripes across it. Louie called it a football field. People walked their dogs there, and we had a blast making fun of the mangy mutts. It was a hoot. I had friends. I had my Katie. She was my girl. The one who loved me and let me sleep on her pillow at night. Tom, Katie, Louie . . . my world was wonderful.

Then . . . my world started to fall apart.

Louie got smushed by a speeding car. Katie went off to this place called college. I didn't like college. I wished she would come home. I wished she'd taken me to college with her. Then, worst of all . . .

Tom moved away!

I was never so lonely. I didn't have a friend left in the world.

When new people came to live in Tom's house, they brought two cages with animals inside. I just knew they were cats! So I raced over and waited in the pecan tree for the people to let them out. I can still remember how startled and scared I was when these two fufu poodles came flying out of those cages and tried to jump up in the tree to eat me. It was terrifying!

For three days I stayed in the trees. Three days, in the cold and snow, with no food or water. Finally I tried to leap to the back fence. I didn't make it. When I landed in the Rotten Willy's yard, I knew I was a goner.

But instead of eating me, Willy rescued me. He plopped me in his water bowl to revive me and give me a drink. He shared his food with me. He even kept me in his doghouse so I wouldn't freeze to death. And after that . . .

Suddenly something yanked my tail. It yanked me out of my daydream, too. It hurt. Claws out and paw raised, I spun sideways to see what had me.

"Willy, why are you standing on my tail?"

The sound of a car horn made my legs stiff. The hair on my tail tried to blow up like a balloon—only Willy was standing on it. Tires whizzed past, right in front of my face. The wind jiggled my whiskers. Willy glared down at me.

"What is wrong with you, Chuck? Ever since your friend Louie got smushed, you've always been real careful about crossing the street. Didn't you see the car? What were you thinking? You act like you were a thousand miles away."

I looked at Willy. The big lug's enormous paw pinned my tail to the ground. I glanced at the car. It had just missed me. One more step and I would have been smushed flat.

Willy was a dog. He looked like a dog. He smelled like a dog. Sometimes he even acted like a dog. Cats belong with cats. Dogs belong with dogs. It's just the way things are.

But even if he was a dog . . . Willy was still my friend. The world just wouldn't be right without the big, ugly beast.

Then again—those first few weeks of our friendship, I *did* spend a lot of time in Willy's water bowl.

CHAPTER 3

Don't remember," he answered with a shrug of his ears. "I think the first time I had to put you in my water bowl was when you fell out of the pecan tree and landed in my yard."

I nodded. "That's the time you saved my life. I was cold and starving and about to die of thirst. Now, the others . . . I don't know if they count."

He frowned and sort of twisted his mouth up on the side. "Then there was that time we were playing tag and you ran into the fence."

"I didn't run into the fence. You knocked me into it."

"Whatever." Willy wiggled his brown eyebrows. "Then the next time was when you were shoving my rump and trying to push me over the fence so we could go explore. I slipped."

My eyes rolled. "I could never forget that one."

"And the time you stuck me with your claws and I jumped. The gate clunked you in the head, remember?"

My whiskers twitched. "I don't remember that one very well. The only thing I remember was waking up in your water bowl." Just the thought of it made me lift a paw and flip it back and forth, like I was trying to shake the water off. "What was the deal with that water bowl, anyway? Seems like, when we first started hanging out together, I spent most of my time in the water."

Willy's stub tail gave a little wag. "Well, you were always getting knocked out. Putting you in my water bowl seemed like the quickest way to bring you around."

Now my other paw came off the ground and flipped back and forth. I didn't even think about it. It just sort of flipped all by itself.

"You threw me in the water so much, I thought I was going to grow webbed feet."

Willy smiled down at me. I couldn't help but smile back. We strolled past my house and crossed the alley. Suddenly Willy stopped.

"Man, would you look at that. There's another house going up. I can't believe it."

With a sigh I stopped and went back to stand beside him. "Me, neither. It wasn't that long ago, we used to come here to catch field mice."

Willy's stub tail wiggled back and forth. "Yeah. You taught me how to pounce. I wasn't very good at first, but I finally got where I could land on them."

My whiskers shot straight out to the sides. "You landed on them, all right. Trouble was, every time you pounced—you totally flattened the poor things. I mean . . . what fun is it to catch a mouse if you don't get to play with it? You can't play with a mouse who's smushed as flat as a pancake."

Willy nudged my shoulder with his nose. It was a nudge to Willy, but as big as he was, his nudges always sent me staggering. I got my balance and scooted back. The smile stretched clear across his big, ugly face.

"I was a lot better at catching mice than you were at chasing cows over at Farmer McVee's."

"There is a little difference in size, Willy," I explained. "You go roaring out in the field, bouncing around and barking with your deep voice—the cows take off. I go out and meow at them . . . shoot, they don't even see me. It's a wonder I didn't get trampled."

In a gap between two of the new houses that were going up, we could see the pecan trees. That's where Farmer McVee and his cows lived. Crows came to the trees to steal his pecans, sometimes. When the fall mornings were crisp and clear, we could hear their shrill calls.

All at once Willy froze dead in his tracks. Kind of crouching down, he motioned with a jerk of his head. I tried to see where his eyes were focused—tried to see what made him stop. There was nothing. Nothing but bare dirt where the men had cleared yet another place to stick a house.

"What?" I whispered. I was so still, my tail didn't even twitch. "What is it, Willy?"

He sprang from his crouch and trotted on. His little, stub tail wiggled back and forth like a sawed-off flagpole.

"Oh, nothing." He chuckled. "Just thought I saw one of those black-and-white kitty cats."

Eyes tight, I watched his fat rump sway from side to side as he strutted down the alley. My back arched. My rear pulled around until it and my head were pointed in the same direction. Bouncing and hopping sideways, I attacked. He let out a little yelp when I latched on to his left hind leg. His whole, plump, rear end sort of gave a hop and came up off the ground. I wrapped around that leg and hung on for dear life. I didn't stick my claws out. When I bit him, it wasn't hard. It was a play bite.

Willy raised his hind leg and stomped. I hung on. He flopped down on his right side and lifted the leg I was all balled up on. I clutched it tighter. He gave it a shake. When I didn't come off, he shook harder.

Next thing I knew, I was upside-down against the neighbor's trash can. But instead of hopping back to my feet and bouncing sideways to attack again, I just lay there. Willy hurried over. He stared at me a moment. When I still didn't move, he leaned down and sniffed. That huge nose felt like the time I got tangled up with the Mama's vacuum cleaner.

"Chuck? Chuck, are you all right? I didn't mean to hurt you. I thought we were just playing. Chuck? Chuck?"

I peeked at him out of one eye.

"Got ya."

Willy's big brown eyes tightened to tiny slits in his huge black face. His snort ruffled my fur.

"That wasn't nice. You scared me. Come on and get . . ."

He stopped what he was saying. I couldn't help but notice the sly twinkle in his tight eyes.

"Come on," he repeated. "Get *up* . . . Chuck."

I flipped over and hopped to my feet. "Don't start that Upchuck stuff with me," I warned. "You know how bad that ticks me off."

He gave a little snort. Well, it was a little snort for Willy. For me, the wind that came was almost enough to roll me back against the trash can. He turned and trotted off.

"I'm hungry, Chuck. Come on."

When we got to Luigi's Italian Restaurant, Willy used his nose to knock on the screen door. A smil-

regular size bowl for me. He plopped them down in front of us, held his tummy, and laughed when we practically climbed into the bowls to get at the fantastic meal.

I loved Luigi's laugh. It was almost as nice and heartwarming as his spaghetti and meatballs.

The trouble with eating at Luigi's was that sometimes it was hard to make it back home.

CHAPTER 4

Willy and I didn't make it home.

"I think I'm gonna blow up." Willy lay on his back in the tall grass. It was the only place on the whole block behind my house where there was still grass. Every place else had been cleared off for new houses. Willy squirmed and wiggled, scratching his back on the ground. "I think I'm gonna blow up," he repeated.

I curled into a ball beside him. Not near enough so that he'd smush me with all his rolling and scratching, but close. I clutched my tummy with my paws.

"Think I'm gonna blow up, too." I licked a little of the leftover spaghetti sauce off my whiskers. In the distance I heard sort of a roaring, rumbling sound. I guess Willy heard it, too. Frowning, Willy and I both listened.

24

The roaring came closer.

We watched as this huge truck came around the corner. It had a big box on the back. It stopped in front of one of the houses. Three men got out. They stretched. They scratched, just like the boys did who were playing with the ball. Then they just stood around.

It wasn't long before a car drove up. A man, a woman, and a little girl got out. The man went to talk with the three guys beside the big truck. The woman and the little girl opened the front door of the house. The three men started carrying things from the big box on the back of their truck. They brought cardboard boxes, three couches, tables, chairs, lamps, and all sorts of stuff.

The man and woman opened the back of their car and began carrying things into the house, too. The little girl reached in the back seat. I felt my eyes get big and round. They almost popped out of my head when I saw her carry this box into the garage. It was made of blue plastic and had a wire front.

It was the same box my friend Tom left in! Yes! Just like the box Tom's people put him in. Was it . . .

No, it couldn't be.

But maybe . . .

My eyes got even bigger. There was something furry and fuzzy inside. It moved. It wiggled. It was something alive. But I couldn't make out what it was. As soon as the little girl put it down, she came back and got another box.

For an instant I was so excited that I could hardly stand it. But . . . these people *were not* Tom's people.

Willy stretched and shook. Standing as close as I was and as big as he was, his shake felt like an earthquake beneath my feet.

"I got to get home." He smiled down at me. "It's about time for my people to come in from work. Let's go. We can play tag or something until they get there."

I looked at my friend. I looked back at the little girl and the plastic boxes with the wire fronts.

For an instant I thought about telling Willy that I couldn't come to his house because I needed to get home, too. If I stayed here and watched . . . if there were cats in the blue plastic boxes with the wire fronts and if they were nice cats . . . well, I really wanted to stay.

But . . . Willy was my best friend. A cat just doesn't lie to his best friend.

The next afternoon I crouched beside Willy's house. He left the bush near the back fence and strolled to the pecan tree. Head high and nose wiggling to sniff the air, he circled it. With him on the far side of the tree, now was my chance. I darted from my hiding place beside his house and shot behind the air-conditioner thing.

Willy always checked the bush at the back fence, the pecan tree, his house, and then the air conditioner. Always the same pattern. Always in the same order.

If I was quick and timed it just right, I could make my next break when he went around the opposite side of his doghouse. From there he couldn't see me shoot across the yard and scamper up the tree. He'd follow the path again, and if I stayed really still . . . well, he'd already checked the pecan tree, so he wouldn't even think I was back there. The dumb mutt would do it over and over. He'd keep circling and circling and . . .

Suddenly a familiar smell tweaked my keen nose. It made my whole body freeze. I didn't move so much as a muscle.

Not far from where I hid, a pipe ran from the air-conditioner thing and into the people house. It was wrapped with some kind of black, rubber stuff, and there was a gap or crack in the brick where it went into the house. My eyes tightened. My tail wanted to twitch, but I kept it still. I didn't even wiggle my whiskers. It was the smell of . . .

Mice!

A sound came. It was so soft and faint that only the sharpest ears could pick it up. Scratching—tiny claws scraping on brick. I squinted at the hole around the black pipe. Held my breath. Every muscle tensed, ready to pounce.

"Watch it," a little squeak warned. "I haven't seen that stupid cat today, but the big dog might be out there."

A single whisker appeared, then disappeared.

My body took over. It wiggled me into a crouch. Almost flat against the ground, every muscle was tight as a steel spring. The instant that mouse slipped from the hole, *he was mine!* Whiskers appeared once more, followed by a tiny, wiggly black nose. It twitched a couple of times, then drew back into the safety of the hole. I didn't blink.

"All clear," the little squeak said. "I'll be back in just a second."

Sure enough, here he came. He shot from the hole. He only got about three steps toward Willy's food bowl when my steel-spring muscles began to uncoil. My aim was perfect. My pounce—stealthy and quick. There was no way he could escape my . . .

Something hit me!

My eyes flashed. What was it? I'd been attacked from behind. A hard nudge or push, right against my bottom. And . . . it came at the exact same second that I pounced.

Suddenly my well-aimed and next-to-perfect pounce sent me tumbling out of control. My tail spun round and round. My paws and claws grabbed for something—anything. There was nothing but air.

Spinning and flopping in an out-of-control somersault, I saw the blue sky. I saw the ground and the mouse. I saw the blue sky again. I saw the ground and the mouse. This time he looked up at me. For just an instant I noticed the terrified expression on his face. I saw the blue sky a third time. I saw the ground and *no mouse*. But I did catch a glimpse of the mouse's tail as it disappeared back inside the hole. Then . . .

I saw stars.

That's because I landed smack-dab on my head. I hit the hard ground, bounced a couple of times, and ended up against the side of the house with my feet and tail sticking straight up in the air.

Startled, stunned, and a little dizzy, all I could do was lie there. The way I landed with my butt up against the wall, my tail drooped down between my hind legs. The tip of it rested on my nose. I could see blue sky on either side.

All at once the sky grew dark.

This huge, black head blocked the light. Brown eyebrows scrunched down to a worried frown. An enormous mouth opened. All I could see were white teeth surrounding a gigantic bottomless cavern. It moved closer.

"Willy!" I managed to hiss. (It was really hard to

hiss, since I was upside-down with my neck scrunched so my chin was against my chest.) "Willy, if you pick me up in your mouth and try to drop me in your water bowl, so help me . . . I'll claw you to shreds!"

The enormous cavern made a *clunk* sound when it snapped shut. Soft, worried brown eyes studied me for a moment. They blinked.

"I didn't mean to tag you so hard." Willy sighed. Then . . .

Willy got tickled.

"You should have seen that poor mouse," he said with a chuckle. "I never saw such a terrified look in my life. And you . . . flipping head over heels, sailing through the air and . . . and . . ."

I struggled to my feet and glared at him. Willy tried to straighten up. He clamped his lips shut. His nose pinched tight.

Only, he couldn't hold it. When he let his laugh out, it came in the way of a snort through his enormous nose. The spray made me feel like I'd been hit with a water hose. It was disgusting.

It made my whiskers twitch and my fur ripple.

Willy laughed and rolled and flopped around.

"It's not that funny!" I hissed.

Willy tried to look serious, but I could tell he was about to bust again. "Don't get yourself all fuzzed . . . *up, Chuck.*"

"That's it!" Without even looking back, I trotted

to the big double-gate and squeezed through the crack.

I really wasn't as mad as I pretended. Still, Willy was overdoing it. It might have been funny—but not *that* funny.

Besides, it was time to check in at home—see what was going on there.

CHAPTER 5

The Mama and Daddy were on a conference call when I got home.

That's what Willy had told me it was, one time when I'd asked him about it. For a long time I'd thought the Mama was just talking to herself when she put the white thing, with the long cord, against the side of her head. A few days later the Mama was talking to herself in the kitchen and the Daddy was talking to himself in the bedroom. I finally realized they were talking to each other. That was really strange. They lived in the same house, yet they went to different rooms and stuck the white things against their heads so they could talk. Why not just sit down on the couch to visit, like they usually did?

When I asked Willy about it, he explained that

they really weren't talking to each other. The white thing with the long cord was called a telephone and some other person was speaking with them. Only I couldn't hear the other people. When more than two people got on the phone, it was called a conference call.

Now, Willy was a dog. It's common knowledge that dogs are simply not the brightest animals—especially compared to us cats.

For a dumb dog Willy sure knew a bunch of stuff. When my Katie first went off to college, she didn't come home for a while. I asked Willy if college was mean and if it was holding her hostage and wouldn't let her come to see us. Willy told me that college was just a place, and my Katie would come home to visit. She did. Willy knew mouth math—that's like two times two is four, and six times six is thirty-six, and eight times nine is seventy-two. Willy learned that and geometry because his boy used to lie on the bed and repeat his mouth math over and over and over again. He didn't think Willy was listening, but he was.

Willy knew how to read the "talkie-light" on the corner of the busy street. He knew that when it was red and the squiggly things that looked like "D-O-N-'-T W-A-L-K" were there, it said "Stop, Willy." When it was yellow, it told the cars to "Go faster." And when it was green with the squiggles "W-A-L-K," it said, "Come on, Willy. Let's go."

Dumb mutt?

Maybe dogs weren't too smart. Maybe Willy really wasn't a dog. When I first met him, I thought he was some strange animal called a Rotten Willy. Maybe he really wasn't a dog at all. Maybe he . . .

"Yes, Katie. We love you, too." The Mama smiled at the telephone. "Of course we'll be there for graduation."

When I heard the name "Katie," my pointed ears shot straight up. Every thought fluttered from my head, as fast as a hummingbird flutters from a flower. My Katie was the other people on the phone. They were talking to my girl.

I raced to the Mama and rubbed against her as I weaved in and out between her feet. I had to hear every single word she said. It had been a long time since our Katie had been home for a visit. Maybe . . .

"Yes, dear. Oh . . . a boy?" Mama's eyebrows arched. "Not just a boy—a *cute* boy. Okay . . . a *really cute boy.*" With her free hand she stroked her chin thoughtfully. "This sounds serious."

Daddy said something in the other room, only I couldn't understand him. Since they were talking to my Katie, I had to hear every single word so I could tell what was going on.

Quick as a wink, I scampered to the hall. If I stood very still and quiet—about halfway between the bedroom and the kitchen—I could hear both of them.

*   *   *

People are sure strange.

When they finished their conference call, they came to the living room. They wrapped their arms around each other and hugged. Then they sat down on the couch and hugged some more. The Mama laughed. Then she cried. Then she laughed again.

Our Katie was coming home from college. Next week Mama and Daddy would go to watch her "Glad You Ate." The boy she met would already be home from his school. It was a different college from the one where Katie went. His Mama and Daddy lived in the same town where we did. When Katie came home from college, she wanted the Mama and Daddy to meet him.

All that was okay. It was fine with the Mama and Daddy. Then Katie said something and they both yelped into the phone:

"Married!"

From that second on, everything got all mixed up and confused.

As I watched them on the couch, I could sense all sorts of strange feelings. There was a feel of excitement. There was a feel of happy. There was sad. There were all these things and more—all mixed up and rolled together. So Mama and Daddy didn't watch TV. They didn't even talk much. They just sat on the couch and hugged.

I hopped up on their laps to see if I could help. They just ignored me. I paced back and forth for a while, then scampered to jump against the back door.

Willy knew mouth math. He knew bored. (I'd been that before, but I never had a name for it until Willy told me.) He knew college, "talkie-lights," geometry, conference calls. Surely he would know what "Married" was.

I kept throwing myself against the door until the Mama finally came.

"What's gotten into you, you crazy cat?" the Mama mumbled to herself as she flung the door wide.

I shot through the opening. I had to get to Willy's. I had to . . .

I didn't even make it off the porch.

My legs locked up. They stiffened so quickly, my claws scraped as I slid across the concrete. Holding my breath, I froze and looked around.

There was someone here!

A new and different smell. A presence. The hair at the base of my tail tingled. Whatever it was, it was close.

It was watching me!

"Hey, Cat! What are you doing here?"

The meow made my whiskers spring up. My tail puffed. I spun around.

"Who's there? Who said that?"

Movement caught my eye. A fuzzed-up gray cat

appeared at the corner of my house. He strolled toward me. This was my house—my yard—my property. But this guy acted as calm and cool as if he belonged here. My rear end wiggled back and forth, ready to pounce.

I blinked. Then . . . I blinked again.

This guy wasn't fuzzed-up. He was *big!*

He marched toward me like he owned the place. Like this was his yard and *I* was the one who didn't belong. My back arched. He came closer. I turned sideways, lowered my head, and pushed my shoulder forward to protect myself if he pounced.

"What are you doing here?" he repeated.

"This is my yard." I hissed, trying to sound tough and brave. He cocked his head. The whiskers on one side of his mouth went up. My tight eyes watched his every move.

"What are *you* doing here?"

Calm and casual as could be, he marched right up in front of me. He kind of stuck his nose in the air, and looked around.

"I like this yard. Maybe I'll decide to make it *my* yard." He took a deep breath. Now he was even bigger than I thought. "Maybe I'll just chase you away and . . ."

A second voice meowed. It startled me even more than the first. There were two of them. I was outnumbered—surrounded.

CHAPTER 6

Roscoe, would you knock it off with that tough-guy routine!" the second meow said.

Trembling, my head jerked in the other direction.

A second cat appeared. This one strolled toward me from the north corner of my house. It was a girl cat. Smaller than the gray, she was every bit as calm and confident. I fought the shaking in my legs. They wanted to run away. Making them stay under me, I tried to act cool. She looked at the gray cat, swished her tail, then glanced at me.

"You'll have to pardon my brother. He was pretty old when our people decided to have him 'fixed.' He still thinks he's got to prove what a tough tomcat he is."

The smaller cat was black instead of gray. She marched right up to the big, fuzzy monster who

stood in front of me and bopped him on the head with her paw.

"Quit being such a nerd, Roscoe." She shoved her way between us and sat down. Her tail wrapped around her leg. "We just moved in." With a jerk of her head, she motioned to the house across the alley. "We were stuck in these dumb boxes for three days. Our people just let us out this morning, and we've been exploring."

She stood and leaned forward. Her movements were slow and not the least bit threatening. "My name's Rikki. This is my dumb brother, Roscoe. And you are?"

"Chuck," I meowed. Only I didn't really meow. The sound that came out was more of a squeak. I flipped my tail and cleared my throat.

"Chuck," I repeated—this time trying to make myself act big and brave and tough. "I've lived here a long time. I was a boy cat, once, too. I'm just as mean and rough as—"

"I can't believe you two!" she interrupted. Real prissy-like, she spun around and flipped her tail from side to side as she walked off. "What is this . . . a guy thing? I just want to look our new home over, find some nice friends, and see what kind of fun things there are to do. You two want to play tough guy with each other, go right ahead. I'll be out romping and having a good time. In the meanwhile, you two will end up all scratched and bloody and hurt."

Both of us watched as she strolled away. The big, mean-looking gray cat didn't seem so tough. He kind of ducked his head, and there was this real sheepish look on his face.

"She's a little bossy, sometimes." He shrugged. "But she really *is* sweet. She's fun, too—well . . . for a sister."

He took another deep breath to puff himself up. Then he let it out, and his shoulders sagged.

"My name's Roscoe," he purred. "I'm not really very big—I'm a Persian. I got lots of hair, so I just look that way. Get me wet and there's not much cat at all. I'm not very mean, either. I'd rather play than fight."

I licked my paw and washed my whiskers.

"I'm Chuck. Since my friend Louie got smushed by a car and since my other friend Tom moved away . . . well, I'm the only cat in the whole neighborhood. I'm not very mean, either. You want to play? You want to be friends?"

"I'd like that." He leaned over and rubbed his shoulder against mine.

Tails high, we took off. We bounced across my backyard and caught up with Rikki at the alley. I sat down beside her. Roscoe plopped on my other side.

"So what kind of action is there around here?" she asked.

I frowned at her. "Huh? Action . . . what's that?"

She cocked an eyebrow and switched her tail to

the other side. "What is there to do? Are there neat trees to climb? Ponds where we could chase frogs? Are there other cats to make friends with?"

"I'm the only cat in the whole neighborhood. But there's lots to do. There used to be a field, right here where your house is. It had plenty of mice to chase. There was even a skunk who lived here. Over there"—I pointed with my nose—"where those tall trees are—that's Farmer McVee's place. In the fall, crows come and steal his pecans. He has cows. They're these big . . . I mean *really big* . . . animals who have two teeth growing out of the tops of their head. I think they call them horns. They stand around and eat grass and all they know how to say is 'Moo.' Anyway, sometimes Willy and I would go over and chase them."

"Was Willy one of your friends?"

"Yeah. He's the—"

"Willy must be huge," she interrupted without letting me finish. "I mean, if these cow things are as big as you say and have teeth growing out of their heads . . . that Willy must have been one enormous, ferocious kitty."

I wanted to explain about Willy, but I didn't get the chance. Roscoe nudged me with his shoulder so hard I almost tipped over.

"What's over there?"

"Oh, that's Luigi's Italian Restaurant. We'll have to go there—for sure. Only not today. I just ate there yesterday. Luigi is nice and fun and friendly. He makes the best spaghetti and meatballs you ever put in your mouth. But never . . . and I mean *never* . . . go to the road on the other side of his place."

Rikki hopped to her feet, spun around, and raced back across my yard. "What's this direction?" she called over her shoulder.

Roscoe and I chased after her. We sat in my front yard, a few feet from the street.

"Who lives there?" she asked.

"Nobody lives in that one . . . well, just people. Two prissy, fufu poodles live in the house next to it. They're all groomed and fluffed, so they think they're a lot cuter than they really are. They're totally nasty and they hate cats. The next house belongs to Rocky."

"Who's Rocky?" Roscoe wondered.

"Rocky's a Doberman. He's the most horrible, mean, obnoxious animal in the whole world. He's not very bright, though. Jumping against the fence and barking threats is about all he does. Only Rocky can't jump and bark at the same time, so he never really finishes what he's trying to say."

Rikki twitched her whiskers. "How about that house on the corner? Who lives there?"

"Oh, that's where . . ." I suddenly stopped what I was saying. I had told them that Willy and I used to chase Farmer McVee's cows. They thought

Willy was a cat, like us. But Willy wasn't like us. Willy was . . .

"That's where . . ." I repeated, only I stopped again. "A Rottweiler lives there. He's huge! But he's really nice. He's kind and caring and . . ."

I wanted to say, "he's my friend," but for some reason, it just didn't come out. I felt my hair ripple when I cleared my throat. "He's really nice," I repeated. "He's not mean at all."

Rikki stood up and swished her tail so hard that it flopped me on the ear. "No such thing as a nice dog. Sometimes they might act nice, just to make us drop our guard. Thing is, they're mean and sneaky and loud and . . . and . . . well, dogs are just dogs."

"Are there more houses behind the ones where the fufu poodles and Rocky and the Rottweiler live?" Roscoe kind of weaved his body back and forth, like he was trying to see between the houses.

"No. On the other side is a field where boy people try to hit each other with a little round ball. Past that is what my friend, Louie, called the football field. People bring their dogs and walk around the track. Tom and I used to sit on the fence and . . . and . . ."

Rikki hopped to her feet and bounded across the street. "Come on," she called over her shoulder. "I want to see. It sounds like fun."

CHAPTER 7

Rikki, Roscoe, and I spent the rest of the afternoon exploring. There were no boys playing with the ball. The stadium was empty, too. I guess that was because a man on a tractor was spraying something on the grass. It smelled really bad. We didn't stick around. Rikki and Roscoe told me they wanted to come back tomorrow, though.

We watched the workmen, busy and noisy around the houses. They kept looking down at the little tick-tock things on their arms. It wasn't long before they put their tools away and left. We rolled and romped and played tag and chase in my backyard. Just before dark we strolled over to Farmer McVee's and looked at his cows.

Rikki and Roscoe had never seen cows before. I guess they didn't believe me when I told them about the two teeth growing out of the tops of their head. When Roscoe saw them, his tail fuzzed. Rikki's eyes almost bugged out of her head, then they crossed and she took off for home. We followed—tails high, bounding and scampering through the field and grass like frisky little kittens.

When our people called us for supper, we promised to get together, first thing in the morning, and play again. As soon as I finished eating, I curled up on the couch and fell asleep. I was really tired. I didn't even patrol the house that night, checking for mice and stuff. I just slept.

It was a fun day. I could hardly wait until tomorrow.

My two new friends were already on the back porch when the Mama let me outside.

My feet barely hit the concrete when Rikki swatted me on the rump with her paw.

"Tag. You're it."

Both cats darted off in opposite directions. I chased after Rikki first. She was a girl, so she should be easier to tag.

Wrong!

There was no problem catching up with her. Trouble was, as soon as I did and reached out a paw to tag her, Rikki dodged or darted out of my way. She was really quick. I swatted and leaped. Once I even made a flying pounce at her. While I was still in midair, she managed to tuck her tail, flatten both ears, and dart right under me.

Tail spinning, I reached for her anyway. Ended up landing in the grass on the back of my neck. I rolled about three times before I scrambled to my feet and took after her again.

She led me back toward where Roscoe was. I don't know how long I chased her, but her brother was sitting beside a tree, watching. Guess he decided I wasn't coming after him until I caught Rikki. When she dodged out of my way, and I kept racing across the yard—right at him—the startled look on his face almost made me miss.

His eyes got as big around as my food bowl. He scampered to his feet, only he stumbled a couple of times. It was just long enough for me to nail him on one ear and make my escape.

Roscoe chased me all over the yard. Once, he thought he had me treed. That's because he saw me leap up the oak in my side yard. Only when I heard his claws digging into the other side of the trunk, I jumped back to the ground and headed for the rose-bushes in the front yard. I gave him the slip.

How he caught Rikki, I don't know. She was the one who found me, hiding in the roses. Girl cats are sneaky. She strolled up, calm as could be, and asked me if I'd seen her brother. Watching her, as she eased closer, I couldn't help but notice the evil glint in her eye. My muscles tensed.

A split second before she leaped, I darted to the opposite side of the rosebush and took off.

"Tag. You're . . ."

She never got the *it* out. She had her paw raised and pounced just as I ducked behind the bush. She tried to adjust her aim while she was in the air, and ended up smacking into the roses.

"Ouch!" I heard from behind me. I didn't even slow down long enough to glance back.

We played tag until our tongues were hanging out and our sides were heaving for air. For a rest, we decided on hide and seek. Rikki was it first.

Roscoe went in front of my house. I guess he was going to hide in the bushes, but I figured that would be the first place Rikki would look for me. I went in the other direction. Racing straight to the oak tree, I scratched on the bark as loud as I could. I dug and scraped and made a bunch of racket—like I was climbing up the tree. Then quietly I sneaked behind the tree, raced across the alley, and hid behind the trash can in Rikki and Roscoe's back-yard.

It was a neat move. I had a long time to rest and catch my breath before they finally sniffed me out.

Roscoe was it next. Then me.

Hide and seek was fun. The two cats never followed the same pattern—never looked in the same places—when they came hunting. They didn't stick out from behind telephone poles or over the top of bushes like Willy did, when we played hide and seek. It was really a challenge to hide from them or find them, either one.

Playing tag was even better. With two cats I didn't have to worry about getting run over or smushed. We frolicked and played and romped until our whiskers were so high, they almost tickled our own ears.

"Come on," I said, noticing where the sun was in the sky. "I've got a surprise for you. You're in for a treat."

Hopping and trotting and bouncing, Roscoe and Rikki followed me across the alley and to the street in front of their house. There, I looked both ways to make sure there were no cars, then led them across. We passed workmen and places where the ground was bare because they had scraped areas for another new house. I raced across the field and right to the back door of Luigi's Italian Restaurant.

Roscoe's nose wiggled at the air. "Something really smells good!"

Rikki licked her lips. "It sure does." She stayed behind her brother while I went to the screen.

I guess there were a couple of things that messed me up. One—I was really excited about sharing Luigi's wonderful spaghetti and meatballs with my new friends. Two—I was probably trying to show off . . . just a little. I mean, it was really easy, since

Luigi knew me, to get a free meal. I probably wanted to impress them.

Whatever the reason, I just wasn't thinking. Without listening to tell if anyone was in the storeroom, I hopped up on the screen door. I grabbed the mesh with my claws and shook.

Almost instantly an arm reached out and shoved the door. My eyes flashed. The door flung wide. I tried to jump down, but my claws hung in the little squares of wire. The door flew faster. Gritting my teeth so hard I could hear them grinding inside my head, I realized . . .

It was too late!

Clinging to the screen, I blinked a couple of times to get things in focus. Then, still a little cross-eyed, I stared down my nose.

Yep. Sure enough. Just what I was afraid of.

My whiskers were all crinkled.

The screen hadn't fallen shut, yet, when I loosened my grip and dropped to the ground. Rikki rushed over. She tilted her head to the side, studying me. Her eyes seemed to watch mine, trying to see what I was looking at. When she noticed my whiskers, she sighed.

"Don't you just hate it when that happens?"

CHAPTER 8

Our whiskers are really important to us cats. They help us keep our balance. They tell us if an opening is wide enough to squeeze through. Our whiskers tell us all sorts of stuff. They're supposed to be straight and well groomed.

The way the whiskers on the right side of my face got smushed between the screen and the brick wall . . . well . . . they were crinkled up like a wad of paper. Curled and kinky as springs, the whiskers wouldn't straighten out. It threw my whole world off balance.

I staggered from behind the screen. The door made a squeaking sound. Glancing up, I saw a young man standing there. He had black hair, like Luigi, but no fur under his nose. Scowling down at us, his lip kind of curled on one side.

"Hey, Uncle Luigi. There's a whole pack of stray cats out here. Want me to run 'em off?"

From the other room I heard Luigi's familiar voice. I didn't understand what he said, though. Pots and pans rattled. Then, wiping his hands on his apron, Luigi came from the kitchen. The whiskers under his nose went up on both sides when he saw me.

"That's no stray cat. That's me buddy."

He gently nudged the boy with the black hair aside and reached for the door. I stumbled back. (I would have hopped back, only—like I said, my whiskers were out of whack, and it threw my balance off.) Anyway, I moved.

"There's my big kitty cat. How you doin' today? You come for some of Luigi's wonderful spaghetti and meatballs?"

I purred and stepped up to rub my cheek against his leg. When I did, I glanced down. Out of the corner of one eye, I could see my crinkled whiskers. I wiggled them. It distracted me a little. Instead of rubbing my cheek against Luigi's leg, I clunked his shin with my forehead. The impact crossed my eyes.

Luigi didn't seem to notice. He squatted down and rubbed my neck.

"How's my boy today? You hungry, kitty?" He stopped petting me. "Where's my other friend?"

Holding my breath, I cringed. *Please don't ask*

where the "puppy" is. Please—not in front of Rikki and Roscoe. Luigi looked around a moment, but he didn't say anything.

"I brought some new friends for you to meet." I purred. "This is Rikki and Roscoe. They're really neat and fun and . . ."

"Oh, I see you bring some new friends for Luigi."

"I just told you that." I purred.

Rikki flipped her tail. "People just don't understand."

Luigi swooped me up in his arms. Between the squashed whiskers and the sudden weightlessness . . . I felt just a little dizzy. He held me in front of his face and smiled. Then he laughed.

"You a good cat. Bring new friends to Luigi's. You been telling them about how delicious is Luigi's wonderful food?"

"You can't tell anybody that." I purred so loud, I knew Luigi could feel me vibrating. "Words just can't explain how fantastic your spaghetti and meatballs are, Luigi. They have to taste it before they could even come close to believing it."

Luigi's rumbling laugh and his smile always made me feel warm inside. He put me down and rubbed my back once more. Then he went inside.

"We gots a fresh pot on the stove," he called over his shoulder. "Let Luigi make sure is ready."

The young man with the black hair trotted after him.

"Fresh pot?" he asked. "You're feeding the good stuff to a bunch of strays . . ."

His voice trailed off when they got to the other room. Rikki and Roscoe stepped up on either side of me and stretched their necks so they could see inside.

"That guy's weird," Rikki said. "You see all that red gunk down the front of him?"

"Yeah," Roscoe agreed. "And he can't even talk people English. How come he talks so funny?"

"It's an accent," I told them. "Luigi is Italian. He hasn't been here very long, so he doesn't make quite the same mouth noises that most of the people do, who we're used to listening to."

It was just a moment or two before Luigi came back. He sat three bowls in front of us. "Here you go. You kitty cats is going to love this. Luigi makea the best spaghetti and meatballs in the whole world. Eat up. You see."

Roscoe sniffed his bowl and licked his lips. Rikki didn't even bother to smell hers. She just pitched right in.

Purring, I rubbed against Luigi's leg to thank him before I started on my meal. His laugh made me feel good. It made the whole world bright.

"Wonder where is my little-bitty puppy friend, today."

Without lifting my head from the spaghetti, I glanced at Rikki and Roscoe. They were so busy slurping their food, I don't think they heard Luigi. I swallowed the lump in my throat.

Luigi stepped over us. He leaned forward and peeked behind the trash cans. Then he walked the other direction and looked beside the building. "Well, maybe he not hungry today." Luigi shrugged.

The young man with black hair stood, holding the screen halfway open. I couldn't tell whether he was opening it for Luigi or guarding it so we wouldn't sneak in.

"I can't believe you're wasting three bowls of your best spaghetti and meatballs on a bunch of worthless stray cats. Why don't you just feed them leftovers or scraps out of the garbage can?"

The happy pleasant smile suddenly left Luigi's face. His soft brown eyes narrowed. The corners of his mustache drooped.

"This one is my friend," he said, pointing down at me. "These others is his friends, so that make them Luigi's friend, too. Luigi no feed his friends leftovers. Only the best for friends of Luigi."

"But, Uncle Luigi," the boy protested. "They're just stupid cats. You dish all the good stuff out to strays, you'll reduce your profit margin."

Luigi frowned.

"You'll lose money, Uncle Luigi," the boy explained.

"So?"

"Feed junk to the bums who come in off the street or to cats and dogs. Save the good stuff for paying customers and—"

"No!" Luigi's voice was so loud and angry, I stepped back from the delicious spaghetti. "No," he repeated. "Money not important. Money is . . . is . . . a thing. Things not important. Friends what count in this life. Luigi never turn his friends away. Luigi never feed his friends junk. Luigi love his friends. Friends love Luigi right back. Love . . . that is what important. Maybe you get older, you figure this out."

With that, he pushed past the boy and went back to his kitchen. I looked down at my bowl.

Luigi's spaghetti and meatballs was the most wonderful thing I ever ate in my life. I'd already gobbled down about half of it and each bite tasted better than the one before.

Trouble was, all of a sudden I didn't feel so hungry anymore.

CHAPTER 9

One time when I was little, I climbed up on the bookshelf next to the planter box in the window. I slipped and landed in the cactus. It hurt.

Luigi's words . . . what he said about friends and love being important . . . that hurt—worse.

He wasn't even talking to me. He was speaking to the boy who called him "Uncle Luigi." But his words stuck me just as sharp and painful as the cactus needles did.

One time when Katie was in school, she came home crying because some of her friends called her names. The Mama hugged her. Then she smiled and said:

"Sticks and stones may break your bones, but words can never hurt you."

I think . . . maybe . . . the Mama was wrong.

Back then I didn't understand why Katie cried. Now I did. What Luigi said about friends . . . his words, well . . . they stuck me like the cactus needles. Only the prickly thorns were deep down inside of me. Not in my leg or my bottom, where I could pull them out with my teeth. Inside . . . where I couldn't reach. Where all I could do was feel the hurt.

Luigi's spaghetti was marvelous. Superb. Fantastic! It was the best spaghetti and meatballs in the whole entire world. I couldn't eat it. All I could do was sit and stare at what was left in my bowl.

It just wasn't right. How could I be such a rotten friend?

Willy saved my life. Willy shared his food with me. Willy let me sleep in his doghouse. Willy played tag and hide and seek with me. Willy *loved* Luigi and his sensational spaghetti and meatballs.

I didn't even think about inviting him to come with us.

Two days. It had been two whole days since I'd seen my friend. Two days since I even gave him so much as a thought. It made me mad to think about it—mad to even admit it to myself—but I was ashamed of Willy.

Why couldn't I tell Rikki and Roscoe that I was friends with a dog? Why did I cringe when I thought Luigi might ask where my "puppy friend" was?

In the meat sauce at the edge of the bowl, there was a reflection. It was a cat. He was looking up at me. He was an ugly cat. He was a fraidy-cat. I didn't like the looks of him—not one little bit.

He was me.

"Would you slow down, Chuck?" Rikki called from behind me. "We just finished the best meal I ever had in my life, and you're racing off like something's chasing you."

I didn't look back.

"Yeah, slow down," Roscoe echoed. "I'm so full, I'm about to blow up. Where are you going in such a rush?"

I didn't answer. Determined to tell my new friends about Willy, I just kept marching. Across the field, past the workmen, through Rikki and Roscoe's yard, around my house, I never slowed my pace. Not until . . .

At the curb in my front yard I stopped.

There was a stranger! I saw him walking into Willy's house. I just got a glimpse of him, but he wasn't Willy's people.

We don't like strangers. Whenever one came into my house, I was always nervous. I hid under the couch or behind the Daddy chair in front of the TV. Willy wasn't as leery of strangers as I was, but I still couldn't help but wonder if he knew there was someone in his house.

"That's it, Chuck!" Roscoe said. Then he belched. "I'm not taking another step until you tell us where we're going."

"Me, neither," Rikki agreed. "If I keep chasing you at this pace, I'm going to explode. What's up?"

Without taking my eyes off the stranger, I answered: "We're going to meet my friend."

Rikki stepped beside me and rubbed her cheek against my shoulder. "If this friend tries to feed us like Luigi did . . . I can't take another bite of anything, Chuck. I mean it."

"No." I shook my head. "He's not a people friend. He's . . . he's . . . Willy. He's my best friend in the whole world." I looked over my shoulder at them. "I think you'll like him. Maybe . . . not at first. It might take you a little time, but once you get to know him . . . well . . . he's kind of different."

"Different?" they both asked.

I gave a quick nod. "Yeah. Come on."

They followed me across the street and down the sidewalk. Right in front of Rocky's house, I stopped again.

"I think you'll like him. Maybe . . . not at first. It might take you a little time, but . . ."

My own words seemed to echo inside my head. *"It might take you a little time, but . . ."*

That's what they needed—a little time. If I just marched into Willy's yard and he came out to greet us . . . Rikki and Roscoe would totally flip out. I mean, what self-respecting cat wouldn't flip out at how huge Willy was? On the other hand, if we went at it slow . . . if I gave them some time to see how sweet he was and how careful he was not to hurt me and what a cool sense of humor he had . . .

I turned and looked at Rocky's house, then past it to where the fufu poodles lived. The gate at the edge of their backyard was opened.

My whiskers gave a little twitch. It *was* about the right time of day. Maybe . . . just maybe . . .

"You two wait here. I'll be right back."

Cautious and jumpy, I trotted to the gate. I took a deep breath and stuck my head around the corner. The place seemed empty. Step at a time, I eased out into the yard. These poodles were sneaky. If they were here, they could come flying at me from any direction at any time. I kept close to the fence until I was about halfway into the yard. Then quickly I bounded toward the big pecan tree.

Still nothing.

I meowed as loud as I could. I rubbed my side on the bark and meowed again. Then . . . making as much noise as I could, I ripped my way up the trunk to the first limb.

Nothing! Not one single snarl. Not one little yap. No fufu, fluffy-butt poodles came growling and barking and trying to get me.

It was safe. They were gone—probably walking around the football track with the woman people who they belonged to.

I leaped from the tree and raced back for my two friends.

"I don't like this," Rikki hissed. "It smells like *dog* in here."

"Come on up," I meowed. "They're gone. Besides, this isn't even the scary part. You ain't seen nothin' yet."

The two cats followed me up the tree. Once at the right spot, we left the trunk and walked out onto a big limb. There wasn't a breath of wind. I was glad. The huge branch that stretched from this pecan tree went over Rocky's yard. It came really close to another branch. That limb came from the pecan tree in Willy's yard. There was a little space between them. I always hated trying to make the jump when the wind was blowing. Leaping from one swaying limb to another was really dangerous. Without the wind even the leaves were perfectly still.

Walking along the limb, I glanced down at the wooden planks below me. It was the fence between Rocky's yard and the fufu poodles' yard. Rocky was lying near the back porch to his house, guarding his food bowl. When he saw me, his eyes sprang wide.

The sudden roaring and snarling and growling sent a little chill racing up my tail and back. But that was about all. Of course, I knew it was just Rocky.

Rikki and Roscoe didn't fare quite so well. Maybe I should have told them about the nasty Doberman. I glanced back.

Rikki was flat on her stomach with all four paws wrapped around the limb we were on. Her claws were dug deep into the bark. Roscoe's tail blew up like a balloon. He doubled back to the trunk and disappeared.

Yep, I thought with a sigh. I should have told them.

CHAPTER 10

It's just Rocky," I tried to explain. "He's a mean, nasty Doberman. He's just noise, though. Rocky makes a lot of racket, but he can't leap high enough to reach the limb. We're perfectly safe. Now, come down before you hurt yourself."

Roscoe ignored me. Eyes as wide as the bowl Luigi fed us in, he dangled by one paw from a tiny limb up high in the pecan tree. No matter how calm I tried to be or how much I coaxed, he wouldn't come down. The poor little branch almost bent double under his weight. All I could do was shake my head.

"Come on, Roscoe. You're going to fall and get hurt. It's safe. Honest. Come on down."

He just hung there.

Sure enough . . . the little limb snapped.

There was a crashing sound. Branches cracked. Leaves fluttered and fell. Roscoe's tail spun. Claws grasped for anything. He hit one limb, then another. Spinning and swirling and flailing, he finally managed to catch himself on a forked branch about four limbs from the top. Desperately holding on with his front paws, his hind feet kicked and struggled. Roscoe managed to chin himself. At last he got a hind claw into the bark and dragged himself up.

Wide-eyed, he sat there puffing and panting until he finally managed to catch his breath.

"Are you okay?"

He looked down at me and gave a quick nod.

"I'm sorry," I called up to him. "It was my fault. I should have warned you about Rocky."

"Didn't scare me," Rikki boasted, with a flip of her tail.

Roscoe and I looked down at her. Rikki was sitting on the big limb next to the trunk. Dainty as could be, she licked her paw and washed her face. Then she primped her shoulders and neck. "Didn't scare me a bit," she repeated.

Yeah, right, I thought. I might have believed her if I hadn't had to climb over her to get to Roscoe. The way she was flattened out on the limb, with all fours dug in—I don't think a Texas twister could have pried her loose. Now, though, she was pretending to be as cool and calm as could be.

Once Roscoe got himself back together, we made our way to join Rikki on the big limb. I apologized again for not warning them about Rocky. Then I explained how Tom and I always used the limbs as a skywalk over the yards.

"Wait, then follow me one at a time," I meowed over my shoulder. "The jump from one limb to the next is a little scary. If we go one at a time, and wait for the branch to stop bouncing, it's a lot safer."

Confident and brave, I trotted along the limb and over Rocky's yard. Sure enough, here he came.

"I'm gonna get you . . . this time." He snarled as he leaped into the air. "I'm gonna yank . . . you out of that tree . . . and tear you into tiny . . . pieces and gobble you . . . down for supper and . . ."

Rocky couldn't jump and bark at the same time. So everything he barked and snarled was all chopped up.

I didn't even bother to glance down at him when I jumped from the big limb on the fufu poodle's pecan tree to the one that led to Willy's yard.

". . . and I'm gonna drop you . . . in my food bowl and . . . save you for a midnight snack and . . ."

"Your turn next, Rikki," I called back, once I'd reached the safety of Willy's yard.

She primped just a little more, then hopped up and started out onto the limb.

"Oh, boy," Rocky howled. "Another kitty cat.

Now I'll . . . have two cats for . . . supper. I'm gonna jump . . . up and grab your . . . tail and yank you . . . down from there and . . . chew you up. Then . . ."

"Ah, shut up, Rocky!" I hissed.

Rikki looked brave, but her legs trembled just a little. She made the jump, though. Roscoe was not far behind her.

He made it, too. Only once on our side, he stopped to look down at the dumb Doberman. Digging his claws firmly into the bark, he started to bounce. The limb bobbed up and down. Roscoe dangled his tail over the edge and wiggled it.

Rocky's eyes flashed wide. He backed off and took a running leap at Roscoe's tail. At the last instant Roscoe flipped his tail out of the way.

"Darn! Missed!" Rocky snarled. He spun around and took another turn. "I'll get you this . . . time. When I do, I'm going . . ."

Again Roscoe moved his tail. Rocky was running so fast when he leaped, and concentrating so hard on the tail, he almost turned a backward flip in midair.

Rikki laughed and fell against me. Roscoe bounced the limb until it swayed wildly.

"Come on, you dumb mutt," he taunted. "You can jump higher than that. What's wrong? You some kind of wimp or something?"

It made Rocky so mad, he couldn't even speak. All he could do was snarl and slobber and growl as

he leaped over and over again—trying to get hold of Roscoe.

"That's enough," I called finally. "Come on and leave the poor pooch alone."

Roscoe strolled slowly the length of the limb. Rocky was totally furious. I guess he wasn't paying any attention to where he was going, because he ran smack-dab into the wood fence between his yard and Willy's. He hit the board with a bang that sounded like he either cracked the wood or his head. I couldn't tell which.

When Roscoe reached us, Rikki rubbed her cheek against his. "That was so cool," she purred. "You rattled that dumb dog until I thought he was going bonkers."

Roscoe puffed out his chest and flipped his tail from side to side. "It *was* hilarious," he agreed. "I mean, I know dogs are dumb. But can you believe that guy? Just crashed into a fence. Bet if I walked back out there, the stupid beast would probably do it again."

They both laughed.

"You two cool it," I hissed. "Follow me. There's someone I want you to meet."

I turned and started down Willy's pecan tree. Suddenly I stopped. I was so busy watching Roscoe taunt the Doberman, I didn't even glance to see if Willy was there—to see if he was watching us. When I did turn to look, I was shocked.

Willy was no place in sight. A knot clumped up in my throat. A sudden chill rippled my fur.

The stranger!

I remembered seeing him on the front porch of Willy's people's house. What if Willy had been dognapped? What if . . .

Frantic, I leaped from the tree and raced to Willy's doghouse. It was empty. I charged across the yard and looked behind the bush in the corner. Willy wasn't there!

What if the stranger had hurt him? What if the stranger scared him and he ran away? My whiskers drooped. My tail dragged the ground.

Suddenly my whiskers sprang up. The big double gate to Willy's side yard was wide open. My eyes flashed.

Maybe the stranger opened the gate and let my friend out. But why?

Behind me I could hear Rikki and Roscoe mumbling. They griped about the way this yard smelled of dog. I caught something about how disgusting it would be if my friend actually lived here—this close to some smelly old pooch.

I ignored them and raced for the gate. There was an odor there—a smell. One was people. I didn't recognize it. The other—it was Willy. Nose almost touching the concrete, I sniffed and sniffed.

We cats don't have a very good sense of smell. Well, it's a lot better than people's. Still, we depend more on our eyes and ears than on our noses. I couldn't follow the scent very far. It went to the left, though. It went toward the football field.

My tail stood straight up behind me.

Maybe . . . maybe the stranger wasn't really a stranger at all. Maybe Willy knew him and they went for a walk or . . . or . . .

I had to know. I had to find him. The football field. The track. If Willy knew the stranger and they had only gone for a walk, that would be the first place to look.

I bounded across the driveway, down the block, past the field where the boys threw the round ball at each other and scratched a lot. Roscoe and Rikki raced close behind as I headed straight for the fence.

CHAPTER 11

See the haircut on that pink dude? You ever see anything so stupid-looking in your life?"

With a frown I tilted my head to the side. "I think it's called apricot. Not pink."

"Apricot, pink . . ." Roscoe shrugged his whiskers. "Who cares. It's ridiculous."

"Yeah," Rikki purred. "Talk about a 'bad-hair day.' "

I smiled, remembering Tom and our alley cat friend, Louie.

"My friend Tom used to call poodles Tutu Butt, because of the weird haircuts they had."

Rikki was on one side of me. Roscoe was on the other. When I said that, they both leaned into me. They hit so hard, I felt kind of smushed. The way they laughed, I was afraid they were going to knock themselves off the fence.

Their laughter made me feel good. This was fun!

"Know why this guy has such a flat nose?" I wiggled my whiskers at the bulldog who waddled toward us. His master was a short, little, plump lady. She looked a lot like her dog.

"No. Why is his nose so flat?" Rikki asked.

Suddenly a chill raced up my spine. It came clear from the base of my tail and stopped right between my shoulder blades. Then a knot kind of tightened in my tummy.

I can't believe this, I thought. *Here I am, trying to find Willy—my best friend—so I can introduce him to Roscoe and Rikki. And I'm sitting here on the fence at the football field, telling dumb dog jokes.*

"Why is his nose so flat?" Roscoe and Rikki urged when I didn't say anything.

The bulldog spotted us. But instead of barking and charging at the fence, he just wagged his little stub tail.

I felt my shoulders sag. How could I be so insensitive? All dogs weren't like Rocky. All dogs weren't mean and hateful. Then again, all dogs weren't like Willy, either. All dogs weren't kind and tender and caring. In a way, dogs were just like us cats. Some were bad, some were good. They were all different.

"Why is his nose so flat?" Roscoe and Rikki demanded. They meowed so loud, it startled me. I jerked from my thoughts and looked at them.

"From chasing parked cars," I said flatly. There was no fun in my joke. No punch to the punch line. I just said it.

I felt like such a heel.

"Let's go someplace else."

I turned and started to hop down. Rikki and Roscoe scooted together, but they didn't follow me.

"No. Let's stay here," they protested. "Making fun of all these stupid dogs is neat!"

"Hey"—Rikki wiggled her shoulders—"remember Spice?"

Roscoe draped a paw over her shoulder. "Who could ever forget Spice," he meowed. "Weirdest cat I ever met in my life."

"It wasn't her fault," Rikki said. "Spice's people made her baby-sit with that stupid pooch. I think, when they were little, the mother put towels down in the bathtub and made Spice spend the night with it. That was the only way they could keep him shut up so he wouldn't howl all night."

Roscoe nodded his head and gave a little snort. "Yeah, but I don't care whose fault it was. She was still weird. She smelled like a dog. Spice even acted like a dumb dog sometimes. I didn't want anything to do with her."

"It's a shame." Rikki sighed. "I really think Spice was a sweet cat. But I'm with you—no self-respecting cat would spend her time palling around with a nasty mutt." Rikki rippled her fur and shuddered. "It makes me feel all creepy inside, just thinking about it."

Now I really didn't feel good. The little knot that tightened in my stomach was a *big* knot now. It was so big, it clumped up in my throat and made it hard for me to swallow.

Willy was my best friend. But I liked Rikki and Roscoe, too. They were *cats* and cats are cool. I'd had a ball the last couple of days playing hide and seek and chase. Just having someone—someone like me to pal around with . . . well . . . it was fun.

I hoped, when they met Willy, they'd like him as much as I did. Only now I wasn't sure it would ever work. The way they felt about dogs . . . Not only that, but the way they talked about cats who palled around with dogs . . . If I told them about Willy, they'd probably think I was weird. They might not want to be my friend anymore.

I didn't know what to do.

Just as I turned to settle back beside them, a sudden noise from behind us made my tail fuzz.

It was a loud roar—not the roar from a dog or anything—just a wall of noise that swept across the field with such force that it scared us.

We spun to look.

The racket came from the baseball field. When we got here, I'd noticed the boys throwing the ball at one another, just like they always did. I'd seen the people sitting on the cement steps. We didn't pay them much attention, though. We stuck close to the fence so they wouldn't notice us and were so busy concentrating on the dogs at the football field, I'd all but forgotten about them.

Most of the noise came from the people on the cement steps. A whole bunch of them leaped to their feet, laughing and pointing.

That's when I saw it!

The thing was huge. Black as death, except for little patches of brown over his eyes and around his chin, he was enormous. He had something in his mouth. It was round and white.

The gigantic beast raced across the field, holding the little round ball in his mouth.

One of the boys chased after him. He got almost close enough to grab him, when the beast dodged to the side. Another boy joined the chase, then another.

One of the boys made a flying leap and tried to tackle him. The beast ducked to the side. The boy landed on his tummy, and a cloud of dust floated into the air. The people on the cement steps roared.

Before long all the boys were running around the field, trying to get their ball back. Even two of the men with the black suits joined the chase. One time they thought they had the huge animal cornered. He managed to duck and dart and dodge his way through the crowd, leaving a whole bunch of boys flat on the ground in his wake.

People on the cement steps laughed and laughed. A couple of them sat down, holding their tummies. Others leaned or bumped against people beside them. One guy laughed so hard he choked on his popcorn. The woman next to him had to beat him on the back.

"That's the most stupid thing I ever saw," Rikki hissed with a sneer. "Can you believe how much trouble that dumb dog is causing? Just like a dumb mutt."

Willy was having the time of his life!

Then . . . I saw it. A white pickup stopped at the edge of the baseball field. It had cages in the back and a flashing blue light on top. A man got out. He had on a brown shirt and brown pants. From the back of the truck, he picked up a long pole with a rope noose on the end.

It was the pound!

I felt sick.

If I didn't do something—and quick—Willy was going to be in so much trouble. . . .

But if I went to rescue him—to make him give the ball back and run and hide before the man from the pound came—then Roscoe and Rikki would know that I had a *dog* for a friend. They wouldn't like me anymore.

Willy circled out to the far side of the field. Staying right against the fence, he outran the boys. How something that big and clunky-looking could

CHAPTER 12

Willy! Drop it!"

All four legs locked up. His eyes flashed wide. His paws dug into the dirt and grass of the field until they were half buried. His mouth fell open. The ball, all went and slobbery, rolled out and clunked on the ground.

I guess I startled him. I mean . . . I probably looked like twice the cat I really was.

My tail was puffed up about three times as big as normal. The fur on my back and sides stuck out to the very tips. I was *totally* fuzzed-up when I hopped from the fence and landed in front of him. A little dust covered me as he finally slid to a stop.

"Chuck? Is that you?"

Back arched, I hopped sideways toward him.

"Come on, Willy," I ordered with a quick glance over my shoulder. "It's the guy from the pound."

I didn't think Willy's eyes could get any bigger around than they already were.

They did.

Both of us took off as hard and fast as we could run. We dodged between the boys dressed in the uniforms. We ran down one of the long straight chalk lines, hopped over the base, and darted out the opening in the fence.

"Lucky that cat came along!" someone on the cement steps yelled. "Guess the dog would rather chase him than play with the ball."

"Lucky for the ball game," someone called back. "Unlucky for the cat. If that dog ever catches him . . ."

Voices faded in the distance. Behind us, I could still hear the laughter. Then someone yelled: "Play ball!" The sound of people clapping their paws—I mean hands—filled the air.

Willy and I never slowed. He followed me around the ballpark, across the alley, down the sidewalk. We didn't stop until we were safe inside Willy's doghouse.

Even then I didn't know if we were *really* safe or not. That was because the big double-gate to Willy's yard was wide open. If the man from the pound looked in and saw us . . .

The sound of footsteps came to my sharp ears.

Willy noticed it, too. His ears perked and his fore-head wrinkled up as he listened. Both of us lay completely still. We didn't wiggle. We hardly breathed. The footsteps stopped just outside the gate. *This is it*, I thought. *We're caught. We're going to the pound.*

Then . . .

A loud squeaking sound sent a chill racing up my back. One of the gates closed. The squeak came again when the other gate swung shut.

I didn't even have time to huff a sigh of relief when another sight caught my eye. Between the cracks in Willy's wood fence, I saw it. It made my heart stop. A flashing blue light moved from one crack to the next. It finally stopped at the gap between the gates. Willy flattened himself against the floor of his doghouse. I shoved into his side. Held my breath.

Peeking over his ear with one eye, I could see the blue light, clear as could be. It sat there a long time. Then there was the loud *clunk*—the sound of a door slamming.

"Excuse me, young man," an angry and mean voice called. "You didn't happen to see a big black dog and a little scrawny cat, did you?"

I tried to flatten myself behind Willy. There was a long silence.

"Well . . ." a different voice began. "I was at the baseball field a little while ago and . . ."

Willy's head jerked straight up. His little stub tail started to wag.

". . . while I was there, I saw a big dog. He stole the ball and was running all over the field. But I haven't seen him since then."

Willy started to get up. I slapped a paw over his leg.

"Where are you going? Stay put. Hide."

"But that's my boy. That's David." Willy's long tongue flopped out of his mouth when he smiled. His little stub tail wagged his whole hind end.

"I don't care who it is," I hissed. "Stay here until the man in brown is gone."

Reluctantly Willy sank back to the floor of the doghouse.

Again, there was a long silence from the other side of the big double gate.

"Well, here's my card. If you do see them, be sure and give me a call. They're dangerous. Especially that stinkin' cat. The little thing looks sweet, but he's as vicious as can be. I almost had them caught a few months ago. The darned cat attacked me. Bit me right on the . . . the . . . well, if you see them, be sure and give me a call."

"Yes, sir. I'll do that. Good luck finding them."

A door slammed. The blue light moved on, winking at us through the cracks in the fence until it was gone. Again Willy started to get up. I whopped him upside the head.

"Cool it! Make sure he's really gone. Just stay here a while."

We waited until we felt almost safe—almost relaxed—when suddenly the back door to Willy's people house opened. Willy's head popped up, tense and alert. I flattened down behind him.

His tail started to wag, but he didn't get up. I peeked around him. Long people legs appeared at the opening of his doghouse. Fists rested on hips above the legs.

"I can't believe you did that," a deep voice scolded.

Sheepishly Willy ducked his head.

"Stealing the baseball was bad enough. But then you tear off and chase a cat. Willy . . . you've never chased cats. You grew up with Tuffy. You loved that old cat and she loved you. I can't believe . . ."

The people squatted down. I barely got a glimpse of him before I ducked behind Willy. The boy people was the stranger I had seen on Willy's porch.

Behind the enormous dog and in the shadows of his house, I was well hidden. I don't think Willy's boy saw me. Course, I couldn't see much, either. I did see a hand reach in. From this side all I could see were the fingers that scratched Willy's ears.

"Tomorrow is one of the most important days of my life. Your life, too, for that matter. You've got to be on your best behavior. I mean, your *very best* behavior. Please . . . Willy . . . please don't chase any more cats."

He gave Willy a hard but loving pat. Then he went back inside the people house. Willy wagged his tail until well after his boy was gone. Then he turned toward me and gave me a big, sloppy, wet kiss with his huge tongue.

"Thank you, Chuck. I never saw the guy from the pound. If you hadn't warned me . . ."

"No problem," I purred. "You would have done the same for me. That's what friends are for."

I kissed him back. (Dogs really don't taste good.)

"Say, where have you been for the last couple of days?" he asked. "I've missed you."

I told Willy all about Rikki and Roscoe. I was afraid that he'd be mad because I had two new cats for friends. He wasn't. In fact, he wanted to meet them.

"They're not too crazy about dogs," I warned.

"You weren't, either," he reminded me. "At least, not when we first met."

"But . . . but . . ." I stammered. "But what if they don't come around, like I did? What if they never want to be friends?"

Willy shrugged his big ears.

"That's not a problem. You can still have them and me—both—for friends. I mean, you can spend some days with them, some with me. It's okay to have more than one friend."

I felt really good when I got back to my house that afternoon. Willy and I were safe. The man from the pound was gone. And Willy was right. You just can't have too many friends. Even if Rikki and Roscoe didn't come around to liking Willy as much as I did—that was okay. I could still be friends with all three of them.

I walked around the house and went to the back porch so the Mama would let me in. Front paws on the screen, I was just getting ready to knock when something made me stop. I turned to see what it was.

Rikki and Roscoe stood out in the middle of my backyard. Eyes tight, they glared at me.

"Hi," I said.

Neither cat said anything. They just stared at me. Finally Rikki took a step forward.

"What was the deal with that . . . dog?"

The way she said "dog" was weird. She kind of spit the word out, like it left a nasty taste in her mouth.

"That was no dog," I answered proudly. "That was Willy. He's the friend I wanted you to meet."

Rikki took a step back.

"Your friend, Willy, is a . . . a . . . *dog?*"

"Yep. He's a dog, all right. But he's really neat. He's cool and fun to be with and—"

"Wait a minute, Chuck," Roscoe interrupted. "Let's get one thing straight. Rikki and I will never be friends with a cat who hangs out with dogs. If you want us for your friend . . . well . . . you're just going to have to make up your mind."

I tilted my head so far to the side, I thought I might tip over.

"You mean I can't be friends with Willy *and* with you and Rikki?"

"You got it, Chuck," Rikki joined in. "Either us or that nasty dog. You have to decide, one way or the other."

CHAPTER 13

Quiet as could be, I sneaked across the yard. At the doorway I paused. A deep rumbling sound shook the morning air. I peeked in his room. He snored again. The noise was so loud it made the boards vibrate. His eyes were closed tight. Without a sound I stepped over his legs and took a seat near the far wall.

The corners of my mouth tugged up when I watched him. Then with a sigh I felt them droop to a frown.

Ugly!

I shook my head, trying to chase the thought away. Nope, there was no other word. Just flat ugly.

And smell . . .

I blinked. The odor made my nose crinkle and

my eyes flutter. What ever made me think I could be friends with one of *them*.

They're just not like us. They're loud and rude and noisy. They'd just as soon fight with each other as with us. They're just . . . different.

I blinked and looked across the room. A smile tugged at the whiskers on the corners of my mouth and chased the frown away.

Okay . . . he was ugly. So? And maybe his room smelled like a pit, and his breath was enough to eat the hair clear off my head. So what?

Willy was my friend.

I crouched low. Wiggled my rear end into a good pounce position. In my mind's eye I could almost see how startled he would be when I pounced right in the middle of him and . . .

A big brown eye peeked at me. My shoulders sagged. Willy's other eye opened.

"Getting ready for one of your surprise attacks?"

I shrugged my ears. "Well, you were sleeping so sound, it was hard to resist."

Willy sat up and shook his head. Slobbers flew from his floppy lips. "Had a late night. My boy kept coming out here to talk with me." Willy stopped to yawn. "I don't know what's going on. He's really excited about something. But he's worried, too. He's never acted like this. I'm happy because he's excited, but . . . something's going on."

Cocking my head to the side, I kind of nibbled at my bottom lip.

"You know, my people are acting weird today, too. The Mama and Daddy didn't even go to work. They've been cleaning the whole house—all morning."

Willy yawned and got to his feet. Then he shook. Short, black hairs filled the doghouse like a cloud. I darted between his legs and went outside. Willy followed me.

"Did you bring your new friends with you?" he asked.

I shook my head. "They're not my friends. They told me they would *never* be friends with a cat who hung out with dogs. So . . . I told them to get lost."

I thought that would make Willy's tail wag. Instead, his ears drooped.

"I wish you hadn't done that, Chuck."

"Why?"

"Well, I'm afraid I won't be living here. I think my boy is going to move, and I think he wants to take me with him. Only . . . only he's not sure, so I'm not sure."

My eyes popped wide.

"Moving?"

"Maybe."

"Moving away from here? Leaving me?"

"I think. I don't know."

It was depressing. Now, I was back to where I was when Tom left. I was friendless.

Willy and I curled close to each other in his backyard and soaked up the warm sunlight. We talked and remembered all the fun we had together. After a while we got up and played tag. Then we rested and talked some more.

When I got home, I saw Roscoe and Rikki playing chase in their backyard. I didn't give them a second thought. I didn't wish I could go play with them. They probably wouldn't have been very good friends, anyway. Friends don't *make* you be friends *only* with them. Friends—good friends like Willy—they understand and like you, no matter what.

The Mama and Daddy were still cleaning when I got home. I climbed to the back of the couch so I wouldn't get attacked by the noisy vacuum cleaner. I hadn't even relaxed when the doorbell rang.

In the blink of an eye I hopped off the couch and crawled underneath it. The doorbell meant company or strangers. I would see who was there before I came from my hiding place. When the Daddy opened the door, my heart leaped into my throat.

It was my Katie!

Suddenly the sadness I felt about Willy maybe leaving and the depression I had about not having any friends . . . well, suddenly it was all gone. Suddenly the day was the most beautiful day, ever.

They hugged and kissed and talked and laughed. Then they hugged some more. I rushed to greet Katie, too. Only with all the feet shuffling around, I was afraid I was going to get stepped on. So I waited by the couch.

For a time I was afraid my Katie had forgotten me. Maybe she didn't love me anymore.

Then the Daddy said: "Come on. Let's bring your things in."

Katie shook her head. "No. There's someone I want you to meet, first."

"He's here?" the Mama asked as she leaned to peek out the door.

"No. But he will be in just a second." Katie smiled. "Is it okay if his family comes, too?"

"Sure."

"All of his family?"

Mama frowned. "Of course."

Katie rushed to the phone. Her hands trembled as she punched the buttons.

"Hi." Katie smiled. Her cheeks turned a little red. "Love you, too. Are you ready? Okay. Give me about five minutes. I haven't even found Chuck yet." Her eyes flashed when she spotted me beside the couch. "Never mind. I found him. Come on over."

Katie hung the phone up and rushed to me. She

swooped me into her arms and snuggled me tight. I purred and rubbed my cheek against hers.

I could tell how happy she was to see me. It was wonderful that she still loved me. But I sensed another feeling in her. She was worried about something. So worried, she was almost scared.

I didn't have time to think about it. The doorbell rang. The Daddy looked suspicious.

"Were they already in the car when you called?"

Katie gave a sly smile. "No. They were home. But like I said, they live really close."

The Daddy opened the door. Katie snuggled me so tight, she almost squashed me. A hand reached in.

"Mr. Archer? Hi, I'm David Dermott. This is my father, Edward, and my mother, Ruth. And this is—"

"Willy!" I yowled.

Despite how tight Katie was holding me, I managed to spring to my feet and slip through her grasp. Her eyes flashed. A little scream slipped from her throat.

"Chuck!" Willy barked.

I raced toward my friend. Willy tried to race toward me, only he had a collar around his neck. The boy clung to the end of his leash for dear life.

It didn't stop Willy. Staggering and choking, he dragged the boy into the house and across the living room.

We hardly noticed the terrified gasps and shrieks

from the people. We met in the middle of the floor. I leaped to Willy's back. He flopped down on the ground. I was so happy to see him, I couldn't stand it. I crawled all over him, kneading him with my claws.

I guess Willy was happy to see me, too. He wagged. He didn't wag his tail or his rear end. The whole huge, enormous, gigantic dog wagged all over.

"You said you were leaving," I meowed.

"We are," he woofed. "My boy's getting married and is going to live in his own home with his own family. He wanted to take me with him, but he didn't know if I was going to get along with his new wife's cat."

"That must be me," I purred.

"Must be."

The frightened looks from the people finally faded when they realized Willy wasn't going to eat me. Wide-eyed and confused, Willy's boy finally let go of the leash and sat down on the couch next to Katie. While they talked about wedding dresses and plans for the future, I showed Willy through my house.

After a while the whole bunch of us went to Willy's. He showed me around. Then the Mama and Daddy went home. David and Katie decided to go for a walk.

We went with them.

"Hey, Chuck," Willy called. "I got an idea."

I circled back to him. "I bet we got the same idea." We both smiled.

"Hey, there's me two friends. How's my little puppy and my big kitty cat?" Luigi's laugh always made me feel good inside.

Suddenly his eyes flashed.

"Oh, excuse me. I not see you." He held out a hand. "I am Luigi. I know this kitty and puppy belong to someone who love them."

David shook his hand and introduced himself and Katie. She shook hands with Luigi, too.

Luigi swung the back door wide. "Come in. The puppy and kitty come for Luigi's wonderful spaghetti and meatballs. You like, too, I bet. Come on in."

Willy and I had never eaten inside before. We always ate out back, by the garbage cans. Luigi put our bowls under the table where my Katie and Willy's David ate. It was neat.

"You know what would be fun?" Willy asked with a little burp.

"What?" I licked some of the meat sauce from my whiskers.

"It would be fun if Katie and David moved into one of the new homes that they're building behind your house."

"Yeah," I purred. "Then we could come here and have spaghetti and meatballs . . ."

"*Every day!*" we both said, together.

About the Author

BILL WALLACE has had pets for as long as he can remember. He grew up with all sorts of animals around the house.

"Our dogs and cats always got along," Bill said. "Fact was, I just knew they could communicate and tell what the other was thinking."

But a friend of Bill's had a dog who didn't like cats. When he rode over on his bicycle to play, the dog almost got Mike, a Siamese that Bill really liked.

He used that dog for Butch in the book *Snot Stew*. Butch was really a "bad guy." Then a fan wrote and wanted to know why Bill made dogs the villains and told him how his dogs and cats always got along. It was that letter—and the six dogs and one cat that live on the Wallaces' farm in Oklahoma, combined with Bill and Carol's "granddogs"—that gave him the idea for this story.

Don't Miss These Fun Animal Adventures from

BILL WALLACE

UPCHUCK AND THE ROTTEN WILLY

Cats and dogs just can't be friends—or can they?

Iowa Children's Choice Award Master List 2000-2001
Indian Paintbrush Award Master List 1999-2000
Nevada Young Readers Award Master List 1999-2000

UPCHUCK AND THE ROTTEN WILLY: THE GREAT ESCAPE

It's a dog's life—as told by a cat.

UPCHUCK AND THE ROTTEN WILLY: RUNNING WILD

It's not so bad living a dog's life. Unless you're a cat.

 A MINSTREL® BOOK

Available from Minstrel® Books
Published by Pocket Books

2300-02

Don't miss these books by
CAROL WALLACE AND BILL WALLACE
THE FLYING FLEA, CALLIE, AND ME

Callie was getting too old for the job, so the house people
picked me to be a mouser. But I didn't plan on getting dive-
bombed by a mockingbird building her nest...or adopting
the baby who fell out. No joke! Flea—that's what I named
her—couldn't even fly. She was pathetic. I had to help her.
The first step was protecting Flea—and me—from the monster rats in the barn and Bullsnake under the woodpile.
Next, Callie and I had to teach Flea to fly. After all, how
could she stay up North with us when her bird family
was flying to Florida? I know I'll miss my Flea. But she'll
come back—after she's seen the world!

THAT FURBALL PUPPY AND ME

Here I am, a self-respecting kitten just trying to survive
in a rat-eat-cat world, when the humans in my life
start acting crazy. Something about the kids, and
grandkids, coming to visit for Christmas. Mama
accusing me of tearing up the presents. Noisy voices and
grabby little hands. If the grandkids are bad, they're
nothing compared to the gift the kids gave Mama for
Christmas...a puppy! Dumb furball. Everybody is cooing
over this yappy puppy who only wants to play. So I got
him in trouble for tearing up the kitchen. Big deal. Problem
is, I feel responsible. This puppy's headed for
T*R*O*U*B*L*E. How can I save him?
I can't even save myself!

A MINSTREL® BOOK

Published by Pocket Books

2306-01